I0456341

MISUNDERSTOOD

A NOVEL

WALTER HORTON

Chapter One

BIOLOGY 11 IS different today. My rat had babies. It's actually Mr. Braverman's rat, but since I take care of it, I think of it as my own. I clean its cage and take it home on weekends and holidays so it won't be lonely. People think it's weird, or I'm weird, because of how much I care about that rat. Also, I wear a white shirt with a breast pocket and a pocket protector for my pens. I wear such a shirt every school day. I own a bunch of them. Nobody else here wears shirts like mine, because I wear them, and nobody wants to be told, "Hey, how come you're dressing like Walter now?"

The rat is here because it is female and big—very big, about a foot long. Also, it is a new mother, and Mr. Braverman wants us to see the rat and her offspring because this is a biology course and we're supposed to learn about life forms. He won't let us see the babies yet because it's too soon. He isn't here right now, either—he's gone down the hall to make photocopies of a handout. His last words were, "Stay in your seats and remain quiet." So, the moment he left, most of us went up to the rat in her cage, to say hi and see her babies.

I stand there with my hands clasped together, looking at the rat in her cage. I'm short and fat and have my share of zits. The jerks in our class like to mock me because of my weight. I clear my throat and say to no one in particular, "We need to stay quiet, like the teacher says."

Talia, one of my classmates, pushes through the crowd that surrounds the table that holds the cage. People let her get right up close to the rat's cage, because she's bossy and has friends. No one wants to be Talia's enemy. "I want to see those babies," she says.

Nobody can see the babies. Their mother has fashioned a nest and has hidden away her little ones. Talia taps on the cage with her fingernail and calls out, "Come out, come out! We want to see you!" She says to me, "Why can't we see the babies?"

"It's too soon," I say, my face red and sweaty. I have to be polite to Talia because of who she is and the power she has at this school. But I like the mother rat much more than I like Talia, and I don't like Talia's attitude, her tapping on the cage. Some of the meanest kids in the entire school are my biology classmates, and it's been a nightmare. "They all need peace and quiet right now," I tell her.

Some of the things they say and do to me are probably pretty funny, if you're not me. I pretend sometimes to laugh along with them when they start in on me, but I'm really seething on the inside.

Now Talia gets that look in her eyes and she turns to face Vinny, who is maybe the meanest bully in a school that has plenty of troublemakers. The other kids in this classroom don't mind him because I'm the only one he picks on. Vinny is no taller than I am, but he's in much better shape and he knows he could take me in two minutes if it came down to a fight. He ambles over towards me and says, "Who made *you* the teacher? We just want to see the babies." He bends double and peers right into the cage. Then he pounds the table a couple of times.

I look around for help. People look away, even Rudy, who is the only friend I have in this place. I'm on my own with Vinny. My heart is beating hard as I say, "Stop that. You're freaking her out."

Vinny shakes the cage hard several times. He says to me, "You're scaring the little ones with your ugly face. I just want them to come out and play."

I swallow hard. This is one of my worst fears: A full-blown confrontation with Vinny in front of the others, with no teacher around to rescue me.

Talia, her eyes twinkling, says, "I'm going to see those baby rats. You don't like it, fat boy? Too damn bad." She reaches for the cage's door.

"Don't!" I shout, grabbing her hand and pulling it away.

"Dammit!" Talia looks at her slightly reddened hand. "Vinny, did you see that?"

I look towards the door and think, *Mr. Braverman, where the hell have you gone?*

Vinny gives me a hard shove. It's his way of saying, *Back off. I'm in charge here. If you bug me anymore, I'll punch you in the face or kick you in the balls.*

Vinny says to Talia, "Just take off the top of the cage if you want to look at the babies."

Talia nods and gets the top off. She and Vinny smirk at me. I just stand there, my blood boiling now. I feel such a bond with the mama rat and her babies, and it's like I've taken them out in their stroller and someone has come along and said, "Let me see your babies. They're asleep. I'll have to shake the stroller and wake them up."

I can't believe what I'm seeing as the top is off the cage. Bits of wood have come flying out and settled on top of the table. We can see the nest clearly now. The nest is made of cotton balls, wood chips and toilet paper. The mama rat has made these simple materials into a snug, comfy place for her offspring. She amazes me that she can do so much with so little.

Reaching down, Vinny plucks the cotton from the nest. Talia squeals. "Oooh! Look at that! Little baby rats!"

I can't really see what's happening, but I'm sure that the mama rat is coiled around her little ones. She and I are both wondering what these punks are going to do next.

"The mama is getting up. She's checking us out," says Talia, giggling. "She's got red eyes. I don't think she likes us very much."

"Of *course* she likes us," Vinny says. "We're such nice people." I move in closer and watch as he pokes one of the babies. The mama goes after him, but he gets away unbitten. "Damn, she's a mean bitch!" he says with a laugh. "Big bitch, too. She could have taken my whole finger off."

I've seen enough. I push past the others and drape my hands over the cage. "We can't do this anymore. She's scared to death."

Vinny clenches his fists and steps towards me, but then Mr. Braverman comes back. "Everybody!" he shouts. "Back to your seats!"

Most students do as told. But not me. I put the cotton and wood chips back where they belong, then replace the cage. Mr. Braverman asks, "Walter, did you hear what I just said?"

I don't move or speak. At this moment, I couldn't care less about Mr. Braverman. I just stand there, staring at the cage.

The student closest to me gets up and looks into the cage. "Gross! She's eating one of her babies!"

A dozen others come up to have a look. I hide my face in my hands and say, "No. Don't look. She's just scared and she's hiding her children."

The mama has taken one of her offspring to an isolated corner of the cage.

Mr. Braverman walks towards the table. The crowd of students instantly parts to accommodate him. "The mother rat must feel threatened," he says. "That's why she's moving her young." He looks at Vinny, who nods, then at Talia, who shrugs.

The big rat digs into the nest and pulls out another of her babies. I expect her to carry it over to the other one. Instead, she looks up, closes her eyes and swallows it whole.

Our teacher closes his eyes and shakes his head. "Oh, my."

I hear groans and gasps throughout the classroom. I'm not sure which of those noises is mine.

Mr. Braverman shouts at those of us standing, "Sit!"

I am sobbing so hard that I don't even bother to wipe away the tears streaming down my face.

Mr. Braverman reaches over and yanks the Levi's jacket from the back of someone's chair and drapes it over the cage. "Hey, bud!" its owner shouts. "That's my jacket!"

"Too bad."

I keep crying, not making a sound. This has been the worst hour of my whole miserable school life.

The teacher turns to face the class. Some kind of tragedy has just happened, and he seems to feel the need to explain. He clears his throat.

"In nature," Mr. Braverman tells us, "sometimes there isn't enough food to go around—"

"But there was plenty of food!" I blurt. "She had more food than she could eat!"

The teacher ignores me. "Or if the mother feels her offspring are too weak to survive—"

"They were fine!" I cry out. "I looked after them myself!" I poke my finger in the general direction of Vinny and Talia. "They were picking on her. She was terrified."

Vinny smirks. "This is a biology class, right? Rats and people and dogs and cats live and die. That rat and her babies? They are here for us to look at and learn from."

I stand there, paralyzed. I can hear the blood pounding in my ears. I look from one kid to the next. When I reach Rudy, he looks down on the floor. They're all looking everywhere except at me. My gut feeling is that they think I'm just fat, crazy Walter, getting all upset about nothing at all. Then I storm out of the room. I hear Vinny make an onking sound and everyone laughs.

I didn't get one of the teacher's handouts, and I'm sure that Vinny and the others will spend the rest of biology class grinning about my behavior. I may fail this course, but that's nothing compared to what may happen to Vinny later on.

Chapter Two

AS I WALK home, I force myself to think about nice things. I pretend I'm headed out one of the back doors to McDonald's when pretty Kathy catches up with me. "You shouldn't cut class," she says.

"I'm not in the mood for gym," I reply. "Too much running. I'd rather go to Mickey D.'s for coffee and a smoke. Come with me."

She shakes her head. "It's wrong to ditch. Anyway, I like school."

"Why?"

"Because it's fun and everyone is nice to me."

"Well, those are good reasons."

I think that I probably like Kathy more than she likes me, but at least I have her, which is a lot more than other people have. She's a cute girl with long brown hair and dimples. She smiles all the time. She acts and looks happy. I guess she *is* happy, whether she's in math class or art class or in the cafeteria. Maybe she's happy because she knows that nobody will treat her like crap. Her life is full of things that give her pleasure.

"I'm glad that you like it here," I say. "I like it most of the time, not I hate gym."

Kathy adjusts her knapsack and says, "I'll pass on the coffee break at McDonald's, but I'll have lunch with you in the cafeteria. OK?"

I point in the direction of the cafeteria and says, "Today they're serving veggie burritos. That's a good reason to go to Mickey D.'s."

"I brought a crap sandwich from home," Kathy says. "I'll give you half."

Kathy doesn't realize that there are troubled, unhappy people in the world.

I smile and says, "We'll have lunch."

I think that Kathy and I could be boyfriend and girlfriend if I had the balls to ask her out. But I'm probably too afraid of rejection, or acceptance, to make it clear that I want her.

Kathy says, "You're here now, so why not go to class instead of McDonald's?"

"You're starting to sound like Mr. Brett."

Mr. Brett, our principal, is someone I know better than I want to. Mr. Brett knows that I ditch school sometimes. My favorite class to ditch is gym. I'm fat and slow, so nobody wants me as their teammate. I sweat through my gym stuff; I pant and fart. It's humiliating. If the gym coach says, "It's shirts-versus-skins hockey today," and I'm on the skins side, I'll just go back to the changing room, put on my regular clothes and go for a smoke and coffee at Mickey D.'s. No way in hell am I going to run up and down the gym with my fat stomach bouncing up and down and my flabby pecs jiggling for the other boys to laugh at. Sometimes I'll ditch gym altogether. If I wake up in the morning and know that I have gym that day, I may even roll over and go back to sleep without attending school at all. I have passed all my courses in high school so far, and I figure that as long as I pass them all, there's no problem, even if my absences are way up. Mr. Brett doesn't see it quite that way. I'm sure Kathy would rag on me if she knew the extent of my ditching.

Kathy says, "I kind of like Mr. Brett. He's so tall and gray-haired. He reminds me of my grandfather."

"There's nothing grandfatherly about him. He walks around like he owns the school."

"Well, he sort of *does* own it."

"And he never lets you forget it." Then, "I need my coffee break at Mickey D.'s. We had Biology this morning and it was ugly."

I tell Kathy about mama rat and my reaction.

"Rudy was there?" She has to think for a moment. "Is he your friend from Boys' Foods last year?"

Rudy and I had that class together. None of the other students would sit near me, so the teacher paired him with me. We found the course ridiculously easy and tried not to bug each other too much. Did that make us friends?

"I cried in front of everyone. They really shook me up."

"You need to cool off. He'll be back tomorrow, or sooner."

I imagine myself in the hallway. Rudy and Kathy see me as I carry the rat's cage towards the exit door. My head is down, my face red. I'm going as fast as I can.

Kathy shakes her head. "Poor boy. That damn Vinny doesn't know when to lay off. I wish someone had the guts to take him outside and kick his ass."

"Me, too. But the gutsy guy who kicks Vinny's ass isn't named Rudy—or Walter, either. Vinny started flexing his muscles a little in front of Walter, and Walter just backed down." Then, "Maybe I should try to find Walter and see if he's all right."

But then the bell rings and Kathy pecks Rudy on the cheek. She runs off, and he touches the spot where her skin met his. He wonders how it would feel to make out with her. By the time he remembers to talk to me and ask how I am, I'm already gone.

Chapter Three

GYM IS THE last class before lunch. Rudy should show up just as the bell rings for lunch and all the students spill out into the hallways. He would just be another face in the crowd. But he doesn't; instead, he goes into the school through the huge main doors and enter the foyer. Mr. Brett is standing there, as if waiting for him.

"Rudy," he says, "I'm glad you could join us." He takes a sip of coffee. "I'm impressed that you had the courage to come in through the main doors."

Mr. Brett is as tall as a tree and stands as straight as a drill sergeant. He wears dark pinstriped suits and has a full head of wavy graying hair. He takes himself much too seriously, in my view. He says Rudy's name again and shakes his head, like, 'I can't *believe* I've just caught you being truant!'

"I have an excuse for not being in gym. I hurt my leg."

Mr. Brett sips some more coffee. He rarely smiles, but that doesn't mean he lacks a sense of humor. He wants to hear some more nonsense about why Rudy has ditched school. They've had this conversation many times.

Rudy finally says, "I was hanging out at McDonald's, having coffee and cigarettes."

"Did Mr. Kramer make the boys do some running this morning in gym? Is that why you skipped out?"

Rudy shrugs. "I just wasn't motivated to go to gym today."

Mr. Brett nods. "You do seem to have quite an issue with 'motivation.'"

The main foyer and the corridor leading to the next section of the building are almost vacant. I can hear a teacher lecturing about something but can't figure out who it is. Doesn't matter, anyway. Down the hallway is the computer lab, probably our school's most popular classroom. Grade 9 boys go in there to look at Internet porn. The lab's windows all have stainless-steel blinds and a pull-down gate in front of the door. They installed the gate so no one would rip off the zillions of dollars' worth of computers. When we have emergency drills, they shut down everything and lock it up.

"You should attend gym as frequently as you would all academic courses," Mr. Brett tells Rudy. "Physical fitness should be one of your top lifelong priorities."

"I hate running. It's hard and boring."

"But you can make it into something challenging and rewarding. It's boring only if you see it as boring."

Kiss my ass. "Yessir."

"People run marathons, you know. They start with one lap around the block. Then two, then three…it all adds up. The biggest achievements start out as very small achievements."

By now they've walked to the cafeteria. It has that rancid, greasy smell that makes me want to barf. Boys' Foods last year made Rudy and me swear we would never eat school food again. A few students are already in line for the veggie burritos, and soon the queue will become much longer.

"Rudy, I don't blame you for disliking gym, but I won't have you skipping out. I won't accept it."

Rudy nods and smiles, as if he'd been threatened with a whipping but gotten only a slap on the wrist.

Mr. Brett's cell phone rings and he pulls it out of his pocket, opens it and says, "Brett."

He listens. His eyes widen, tough tightens, face turns ashen. He mutters, "I'm on it." He hurries off without saying goodbye to Rudy, who whispers, "Later, dude."

Rudy goes off to meet up with Kathy. Wish I could trade places with him.

Chapter Four

I HURRY UP the stairs to the second floor as the lunch bell sounds. Classroom doors swing open and chattering students scramble out into the hallway on their way to the cafeteria. Some of them sit on the floor by their lockers while to eat lunch and have bull sessions. Some guy hustles past me, and my knapsack smacks him in the chest. He shoots me a dirty look, to let me know he's mad, but not enough to punch me out. I spot Kathy at her locker and stand back as Rudy, like a footballer, pushes past people to give her a little hug.

Kathy is pretty in that no-makeup, hippie-girl kind of way. When I get close enough to her, she seems to smell of chewing gum and perfume.

"Mr. Brett is concerned about my physical fitness," I can hear him tell her. "He thinks I should take the rest of the afternoon off and take a long walk."

Kathy giggles. "If you want me to join you, I can't. I have a math class this afternoon, and I'm pretty sure I know everything that's on it. I want an A *so* bad." She opens her locker and takes out her math textbook. "Help me." She motions for me to sit down beside her. I happily do.

I like math much more than other subjects and attend class most of the time. I like the fact that it's objective—for every question, there's a correct answer. I hate English because it's subjective. When our teacher, Miss Creel, assigns a paper for us to write—an essay, composition, book review or whatever—she bases the grade she gives you on how much, or little, she likes you. Therefore, you can write an A-quality paper and end up with a C+, or vice versa. At least in math, even if the teacher thinks you're the biggest doofus ever, you'll get an A if you get all the questions right.

I dread Miss Creel's mean face and nasty voice so much that I ditch English whenever I'm not in the mood to deal with her.

Simplifying fractions is almost fun as I sit there with Kathy. I love it that everyone can see us sitting together, like we were boyfriend and girlfriend or something. I watch as she does math. She does it so fast, and with such concentration, that she obviously likes it a lot. It's fun and games to her.

Kathy catches me staring at her. She smiles at me, her cute dimples deep and dark. If I had the guts, I would lean over and kiss her lips. Girls and their lips and butts and breasts. They drive me crazy.

I tell her, "Math is easier for me than English."

I inhale her perfume. She smells much too yummy.

"Math is the language of science," she says. "Without trigonometry, we would have no engineering. Without engineering, we would have no civilization."

I fantasize about our kiss. How long would it last? Would she like it, too?

"I love math's consistency," I tell her. "No matter what else changes in the world, two plus two will always make four."

"Amen to that." She closes her eyes, as if she wants that kiss to happen.

Then the alarm sounds. It's loud enough to make the floor vibrate.

Kathy groans. "Lockdown time again."

A bevy of girls plops down onto the floor and starts eating lunch as if nothing is wrong. Nearby, some other kids stand around, laughing and carrying on.

A teacher emerges from a classroom. He yells, "Lockdown!" When students just look at him, or totally ignore him, he grabs the nearest small kid and pushes the child into a classroom. Then he dashes over to the bevy of girls sitting on the floor and pulls up one of them by her arm. She yells, "Hey! Watch it!" as he stuffs her into the same classroom the small kid is in. A few others saunter in, too, but many others move slower than cattle.

I get up fast and say, "I guess your math test will have to wait. Do you want to get locked down in here or ditch school with me?"

Kathy makes a face but lets me help her to her feet.

The teacher has gotten the kids' cooperation. He stands at the classroom door, making hurry-up motions with his hands as the boys and girls, in ones and twos, enter the big room. He shouts, "Lock it up. Nobody enters or exits."

It's only a drill and this teacher is on some kind of power trip. I squeeze Kathy's hand and say, "We can still get out through the back stairs. Everyone keeps forgetting we *have* back stairs."

We giggle as we enter the vacant stairwell and hop down the stairs. But when we try the doors on the bottom floor, they're locked. Then we hear Mr. Brett over the public-address system. He says, his deep voice booming, "Attention! This is not a drill. Someone with a gun is in the school."

He is right. I *know* he is.

Chapter Five

I HAVE TO laugh at the images in my head. Suddenly, the whole school seems to remember our back stairs. Kids jump down the stairs and pound on the locked doors. The kick the doors and swear at them, too, as if that would do any good.

"Let's go back up," I say to Kathy. "I know another way." We struggle up the stairs, pushing past people on their way down. They don't know the door is locked down there, and when I tell them, they ignore me. They get to where they're going, curse at the locked door, and soon we're all going in the same direction—up. I keep a firm grip on Kathy.

When we reach the second floor, we find dozens of kids struggling to squeeze through the doorway leading to the corridor that leads to the classrooms. It's like the biggest rock concert in town is about to begin and everyone's fighting to get closest to the stage. So many people are packed in together that no one is moving. Some big dude hurls himself towards the door as if he were in a mosh pit. He's wearing steel-toed boots and he uses people's heads as footholds. But the big dude gets to where he's going, and other guys do likewise. Someone starts trying to climb my back. A girl's Nike catches me in the eye as she uses another kid's shoulders as a ladder. Girls and boys, climb and claw over each other, pull hair, step on heads. They're all desperate to get away from the crazy guy with a gun, whoever or wherever he may be.

"Want me to give you a boost?" I ask Kathy.

She shakes her head. "I'm staying here with you."

Then something up ahead gives way and the way is clear, sort of. It's all I can do to keep from falling on my ass as the students keep pushing and shoving on their way into the classrooms. The girl in front of me trips and falls flat on her face. A few students jump over her, but others walk right on top of her, leaving footprints on her butt and back. At first I want to step around her; instead, I pull her up and slap some of the dust off her back.

Turns out it's Talia from Biology 11. Her hair is messy, her makeup running. She wipes tears from her cheeks. I don't think being stepped on has hurt her physically as much as emotionally. She's just not used to being stepped on, period. It's the humiliation that hurts so much. I know way too much about humiliation. Talia staggers, so I right her again as boys and girls run past us, screaming and crying. It's all so much like one of those Hollywood movies I've seen. But this is no movie. It's the real deal.

I grab Kathy and Talia and force them into a classroom that is already packed with hysterical young people. Some of them cower under the desks, as if that will do them any good. If the shooter wants them, he will get them. Wherever they are, being in the classroom is much better than being stranded in the corridors. People are yelling, "The door's still open! Close it now!"

I put all my weight into forcing the kids ahead of me into the classroom, which is already crowded. I give a hard shove to the kid in front of me, driving him into the classroom. Meanwhile, boys and girls are still hollering to close the door, even though not everyone is in yet. That includes Kathy and me.

The guy in front of me, who is now just inside the classroom, spins around and slams the door in my face. "Lockdown!" he yells.

"Wait! We're still out here!" I yell back.

I hear the click of the lock. Damn!

In the drills, they make it clear that once the door is locked, nobody is allowed to come in or go out. It's for everyone's safety. What they fail to teach is the importance of working together and making sure everyone is in the classroom before they lock the door. But the others have done exactly that, and now Kathy, Talia and I are stuck out in the hallway. I look right and left, seeing nothing but an empty corridor and many locked doors. I kick the door that's just been slammed in my face.

Kathy runs a hand through her sweaty, oily hair. She isn't crying at the moment, but I see dark circles under her eyes. She looks pale and forlorn. She is unused to dealing with bad stuff.

I throw myself against the door and feel it give just the tiniest bit.

Talia screams, "Let us in! He'll kill us!"

She has membership in all the A-list cliques, so if they refuse to open the door for her, they sure won't do it for me. Out of frustration, I throw my body into the door a few more times. Then I feel Kathy's gentle touch on my arm. "Walter, let's go somewhere else."

"Really? Where? All the classrooms are locked, and we're stuck out here because I wanted us to leave school. It's kind of all my fault."

Kathy takes my hand. I can feel the warmth of her touch. I could never get tired of feeling of having her near me.

She says, "Let's go, Walter."

At our feet, Talia sits with her face in her hands. Kathy and I haul her to her feet. We walk away, then run as we hear the first gunshots ring out.

Chapter Six

THE SHOTS SOUND far away, as if from downstairs, maybe the main foyer. Kathy and I walk with Talia behind us, holding her hands as if she were a child. When she wants to stop and rest, I say, "Hurry! Keep moving!"

Kathy shakes her head at me. To Talia she says, "We have to get to safety. Can you make it?"

Talia gives her the tiniest nod.

We move as fast as possible down the corridor. All the classroom doors are locked, but the occupants' frightened voices are audible. *If you're freaked out being in there*, I silently tell them, *just try being out here.*

On an impulse, I steer us towards the boys' washroom. I push at the door and it opens. We go inside.

Barinder, one of my classmates, is leaning against the wall, smoking a joint. When we enter, he hides his joint behind his back.

"Whoa!" he exclaims. "I thought you were Brett. If he catches me getting high again, he's gonna expel my ass." He adds, "How come the chicks are in here? Don't they have their own can?"

"Barinder," I say, "haven't you heard?"

He shrugs. "Tell me."

"We're on lockdown."

"How come?"

"There's a shooter on campus."

He arches his eyebrows. "No shit, hey?"

"You would already know about it if you weren't in here, getting stoned on weed," I tell him.

"Well, I know now. Thanks for the heads-up. You guys in here because you're afraid he'll shoot you?"

"Something like that."

Barinder nods and sucks a bit at his roach, which he then flushes down the sink. "Drugs are bad for you, man. Just say no."

"I hear that."

Just then we all hear some gunfire. This time it sounds much, much closer than the main foyer.

"Time to take cover," Barinder says. He slips into one of the toilet stalls and locks it. He stands on the toilet seat.

Kathy says, "Talia, come away from the door. We have to hide like Barinder." The washroom has four stalls—one for each of us.

We hear more gusshots—*pop, pop, pop*—and we hurry into the stalls, knowing that the shooter is coming to get us.

We lock our stalls and stand on the toilet seats. The room smells of piss and crap, and the chemicals they use to cover up the stink smells worse than the piss and crap. Talia starts whimpering.

"If he can hear us," I whisper, "he'll shoot us."

Talia stops whimpering.

In the washroom, it is so quiet that we can hear the hum of whatever machine is on. More gunshots outside, and more screams from those lucky enough to be locked down. If he wanted to do so, he could probably shoot apart a door lock and enter a classroom, but then he'd be surrounded by a bunch of freaked-out kids, and a few of them might just jump on him and take away his gun. So he's just walking around, busting caps. Getting everyone totally freaked out.

Barinder, Talia and Kathy make themselves as comfortable as possible on the toilet seats. Talia takes out her cell phone and starts punching buttons. When I was thirteen, my parents refused to buy me a cell phone. By the time I was fourteen, they *made* me carry one.

Today, everyone at our high school has a cell phone. So does everyone else on Planet Earth. I'm sure many of them have called the cops by now. Why haven't the boys in blue arrived?

Talia's cell phone makes a bleeping sound when in use. Kathy says, "Talia, you're not seriously making a call right now, are you?"

"Why do you ask?" Talia retorts.

"Because," Kathy says, as if speaking to a very small, very stupid child, "we need to shut up so that the shooter doesn't barge in here and kill us."

"Yeah, I forgot." We hear the cell phone snap shut.

More *pop-pop-pop* sounds come even closer. I shift my weight on the toilet seat and groan. Barinder, in a low voice, says, "Stay cool, dude."

For the longest time it's so quiet that the electrical buzzing of the overhead light is deafening. Then I hear the tiny groan of the washroom door as it's being opened. The screams and shouts of locked-down students, like the cries of condemned killers, become unbearably loud. I'm sure Barinder is every bit as anxious and terrified as I am, but he would never admit to being in a situation he couldn't handle. I want to scream but no sound would come out. Then I hear some goofy canned music. It's Talia's cell phone again.

Yea, Talia! Way to go, girl! Why don't you just yell, "Hey, shooter! We're here in the can! Come and get us'?"

Talia turns off her cell phone.

Sweat trickles into my mouth. I swallow it, wincing at its awful taste. I can hear Barinder's breathing, or maybe it's my own. The hallway gets a bit quieter and I'm sure the washroom door is now closed. Did the shooter leave? With the whole school on major lockdown, there is no one for him to shoot. Maybe he'll just go home.

I hear someone's heavy tread. He's come in. he's checking things out. I can swear I can feel his hot breath on my skin.

My legs turn to mush. I have to use all my strength to sit still and not collapse onto the floor. His footsteps seem to have stopped just outside the row of stalls. I hear laughter, a weird maniacal *hahahahaha*, and then there's this *bang!* A single shot just a few feet away, but it's as deafening as a pile driver at a construction site.

The single overhead fluorescent light shuts off with a feeble flash. Now it's much darker, and after a *rahahaha!* laugh, the heavy footsteps move towards the door and it swings open again.

I'm sweating harder than ever, but now I'm shivering, as if it's the middle of winter and I'm wearing a T-shirt. I wonder if I fed my pets this morning. Probably. Did I tell Mum and Dad that I loved them? Probably not.

Chapter Seven

IT SEEMS OK to scream, so I do. Barinder screams, and so do Kathy and Talia. After a few minutes that seem like a few hours, we unlock our stalls and creep out. Barinder swears at the shot-up light and the plastic shards littering the floor.

"Kathy?" I call out. "Kath—"

"Right here," she says, coming over for a hug.

I give her one.

The silence has returned, so I take a moment to be grateful that I'm still alive. Not dead. Not even wounded. I'm glad...but how come he spared us?

"I'm fine, sort of," Kathy says.

"Me, too." I add, "Well, no, but he didn't cap my ass." My tough-guy talk sounds ridiculous. My voice is little more than a croak.

I hear the familiar flick of Barinder's plastic lighter, and his face glows above its flame. "Not sure why he hit the lights."

The light coming in through the window is much dimmer as we four stand facing each other. It's like we're waiting for the moment that one of us will say or do the thing that will make our daytime nightmare go away. I turn to look at Talia. "Looks like you're bleeding."

She frowns, then puts her hand to her head. She holds her hand close to her nose. "I smell blood."

"Better sit down," Barinder says.

Talia starts to wobble, as if she's about to faint, so I grab her and ease her to the floor. Kathy rips some paper towels from the dispenser and presses them to Talia's head.

Talia begins whimpering.

I'm hardly an ER doctor, but I have a feeling she isn't hurt that badly. Mostly, she's just freaked out and in shock. So am I, come to think of it.

"Barinder," I say, "hold the lighter closer to us."

"Maybe," he says, "I should open the door to get more light—"

"No!" Kathy and I shout.

Barinder holds the lighter as close to Talia's head as he can without making her feel too hot. The wound seems to be somewhere above Talia's left ear. I run my fingers around her scalp with a doctor's businesslike manner and decide that, apart from the small wound, she's OK.

"I think a piece of plastic may have gotten a bit of your scalp," I tell her. I could have added, "At least the bullet didn't enter your skull and spatter your brains all over this washroom."

Barinder pulls off his sweatshirt and helps Talia into it. "Gotta keep you nice and warm." He then puts his arms around her.

I'm really surprised at Barinder's Good Samaritan gesture, and so is Talia, but she nods and relaxes against him, whimpering. I figure out now that she's pissed her pants, but none of us says anything about it. Talia takes out her cell phone and starts dialing a number.

"I think," Kathy says, looking at Talia's scalp, "that the bleeding has stopped." She hands more paper towels to Barinder, who applies them to Talia's head. Kathy stands up and puts her hands on her hips.

I pull her into my arms and dig my face into her hair. When I pull back, I can see tears streaming down her face. "What's up with those tears?"

"Three guesses," she says, wiping her face.

"He's gone now. He had his chance, but he let us live."

"Poor Talia."

"She'll be fine. We'll be fine."

Barinder shakes his head. "This is all too freaky. He came in here, shot the light but didn't shoot us. Why not?"

I can picture the expression on Walter's face when he entered the washroom and saw us. Happy. Victorious. Then I saw his look change when he recognized me. He was, like, *Oh, it's you. I can't kill you because you're the closest thing to a friend I have in this school. That's too bad.* Then he took off.

"The shooter's name," I tell them, "is Walter Horton. He's somewhere else in the school right now, doing to others what we thought we was going to do to us."

Chapter Eight

WHY IS EVERYONE looking at me like that? Staring, as if I could have prevented Walter from coming to school with a gun.

Kathy steps away from me. "You mean Walter, the rat guy from Mr. Braverman's class?"

Talia groans.

Baruider asks, "Who is Walter Horton?"

Barinder, Walter and I are all the same age, in the same grade. "You've seen him lots of times. Fat kid, high-and-tight haircut. He wears nerdy glasses and a white shirt with a plastic pocket protector."

He shakes his head. "Don't know him." Barinder's into being an Indian James Dean—way too cool to let on what's bothering him, never very affected by good things or bad. As a cool kid, he would never admit to knowing the Walter Hortons of the world.

"You know Walter," I say. "You just won't admit it. Well, he's here today and he's got a gun."

Barinder says, "My dad has a gun. He keeps it in his car's glove box in case he needs it for self-defense."

"Does he have a permit for it?" I ask.

"I don't think so," he says.

"He better hope the cops don't catch him with it in his car. He could go to prison for that."

"Yeah, I'll be sure to tell him you said that." Then, "Anyway, Walter's gone and maybe he won't be back."

Kathy eyes me. "Do you know anything about this?"

"Like what?" I ask. "You think Walter came up to me and said, 'I'm gonna go to school and shoot some people'?"

But I recall the way Walter looked at us in the classroom, how he seemed to feel that everyone was picking on him. He was like, 'I'm gonna get you bastards for this.' I swallow hard and blow out a big sigh.

Talia starts frowning. Maybe she's thinking the same things I am. "Vinny is such a creep. He was tormenting that rat in science class. That's what got Walter so upset. Vinny gets away with *so* much shit."

"Victor *is* a mean, nasty kid," I say. "But you're not much better, and I've seen you and him hassle other kids together and then laugh about it afterwards.

"You weren't exactly being Miss Congeniality with that rat this morning," I tell her. "You could have said, 'Vinny, that's enough. Stop it.'"

Talia's mouth drops open. "Excuse me? Are you saying that this shooting thing is somehow *my* fault? Uh, I don't *think* so. You want to know why Walter's walking around out there with a gun? It's because he's crazy, and I didn't make him crazy. He's like Lady Gaga. He was born that way."

I shake my head. "I'm not saying any of those things. What I *am* saying is that Vinny subjected Walter to more than the usual amount of cruelty, and Walter snapped. Someone should have stood up to Vinny and told him to back off." I add, "Walter isn't crazy. He's just…misunderstood."

Barinder says. "Whatever."

Kathy glowers at him. "You *agree* with him? Walter's out there with a gun and he's just 'misunderstood'?"

Barinder puckers his lips. "Well, I'm not saying that I'm the shoot-'em-up type, but haven't you ever wanted to get even with someone by blowing them away?"

"God, no."

Talia smirks. "I've killed lots of people in my daydreams. I felt better afterwards."

"Let's be heroes today," I tell them. "Let's go tackle Walter and take his gun away."

Kathy shakes her head. "No can do. He'll shoot us before we can tackle him."

"Do you remember that shooting spree in the States ten years ago?" I ask. "The shooter? Kip Kinkel? They tackled him to end the shooting."

"Actually," Kathy says, "they tackled him because he was having trouble reloading. His gun got jammed or something and his hands were shaking, so the other kids said, 'He can't reload. Let's get him.' That situation was different from this one."

I shrug. "Guess you're right." I add, "Still, I just feel like we should do something."

Kathy says, "Not us. He has a gun, but we don't. This is for the cops. They have to deal with this, not us."

"But if we don't get to him, the cops will shoot him or he'll kill himself."

"So what's the problem?" Kathy asks. "Those two Columbine school kids who shot up their school? Their last two victims were themselves. It was either that or life in prison. They made damn sure they killed themselves. Kip Kinkel survived because they other kids jumped him before he could shoot himself. He's like, thirty now and has been in the slammer since Nineteen Ninety-eight. To this day, he regrets that he didn't have the chance to kill himself. I'm sure Walter Horton must be thinking, 'They'll never take me alive.'"

Kathy's practically spitting with rage, and I can totally empathize with her. There's no way anyone can defend Walter's actions. But think of all those times people have degraded him! Even our guidance counselor doesn't know how bad the persecution has been.

"Some people go through their whole lives being abused," I say to Barinder, Kathy and Talia. "You don't know what Walter has endured."

"I don't *want* to know about it," says Barinder.

"We can't relate to him because he's, you know, not exactly like us," I say.

"I know," Kathy says. "We don't come to school with guns to get back at those who have wronged us."

"He didn't shoot any of us. He shot the light. Maybe I can find him and talk to him. We can have a talk in a way that kids can't have with parents or shrinks or social workers. We can talk like friends."

Kathy says, "You sound like you're on *his* side."

I guffaw. "Whose side am I on? I'm on the side that wants to restore peace and order to this high school."

"Think about this very clearly," she says. "There is a kid out there with a gun. He's probably killed some people this morning, and he'll probably kill some more before he kills himself. Are you really going to find him and say, 'Put the gun down, Walter. Let's have a chat about your personal issues'? You think that will get you anything but shot?"

Then we hear a few more gunshots.

"Yeah," Kathy says. "Go talk some sense into him."

The sound of that gunfire makes my pulse speed up. "Kathy, it's something I have to do."

She taps her temple and says, "He's got problems up here, you know? That's why he's out there. If you go out there and try to get him to hand over his gun, you're no better than he is. We'll just wait it out in here. The cops will come along and deal with him."

I arch my eyebrows, not knowing what to say to her. Our friendship, for the moment, has gone bad. Maybe later on we'll make up.

Barinder, who seems to feel that I've made up my mind to go out and confront Walter, says, "If I was the gunman, I would head for the cafeteria. Lots of people will be there."

"Right," I say.

"Wrong," Kathy says. "We're in lockdown mode, remember? That's the first place they closed."

I think back to Boys' Foods last year, and how much fun I had exploring the supply hall behind the kitchen. In that part of the school, it's really a maze; the kitchen, supply hall, theater concession and theater are all linked together. When they're holding special events in the theater, like plays or musical performances, they sell coffee, pop and goodies in the concession. Right now, there's nothing going on, so they use the concession as a big storage area for props and whatever. They wouldn't have locked the concession because most people keep forgetting it's there. One time in Boys' Foods, I started out in the supply hall and found my way into the darkened theatre. I spent a long time there, safe from all the bullies, and enjoyed every moment. I wished I could have brought a sleeping bag with me and made that place my new home.

"Walter could probably get into the cafeteria," I say. "He knows the ins-and-outs of this school. Some of the doors don't have locks. One of them leads to the kitchen, which of course leads to the cafeteria."

"So he knows all the little nooks and crannies here?" Kathy asks. "Why does he know that?"

"I guess he has his reasons."

Barinder gives a small, bitter laugh. "So the guy knows the layout of this school. The cops will never find him."

Talia snorts. "The cops will never find him because they're too busy having coffee at Starbucks."

I laugh in spite of myself. "I'm about the only one who could find him at this point. I know this school's hidden places as well as he does."

Kathy looks about ready to cry. "Maybe you'll be too late."

"But maybe I'll be just in time."

Chapter Nine

AS SOON AS I exit the washroom, my fantasy ends and I become Walter Horton again. I am the laughingstock of this high school, not the friend who hugs Kathy, helps Talia with her little head wound and is on decent terms with Barinder. In real life, Barinder wouldn't condescend to spit on me.

After what happened with the rats this morning, I went home and got my father's nine-millimeter Glock handgun and a few magazines of extra ammo. Then I returned to school.

Of course, from the moment I stepped into the main foyer, everyone saw me and my Glock and ran like hell. It was like so many movies I'd seen: *There's a killer on the loose, run for your life!*

What nobody knows is that I'm scared, too. This armed visit to school is something that's been on my mind for quite some time. Now that it's actually happening, a part of me wants to call it off and run back home.

But I don't.

The main foyer, and the corridor connected to it, are deserted. Someone's brown lunch bag here, and a Coke can there, remind me that people were doing their usual thing when the lunchtime-lockdown panic happened. Being here now, I stay close to the wall, so that if the cops storm this area, maybe I'll be a more difficult target to hit.

The theatre, which is where I want to go, is at the other end of campus, but that's no problem. At a corner, I stop and peek around, to make sure the cops haven't arrived.

I half-run through one corridor after another, past more lunch bags and flung-open lockers and locked classrooms. The locked-down students are silent. Or maybe they're screaming and shouting. I can't hear anything except my own heartbeat.

I reach the theatre's big brown double doors. If they're unlocked, I can go in. If they're locked, I'm going to have to run back to the main foyer, then go to the gym and machine shop, to the other hidden passageways into the theatre.

I try the theatre door, hoping it's unlocked. I'm too fat for all this running-around shit.

The door opens. I go inside.

The theatre is one of my favorite places in the world. I like how big it is, how dark and quiet. I imagine myself on that big, gleaming stage, performing for a sanding-room-only audience. Then I bow and smile as I receive a standing ovation.

I remember how much time my friend Rudy and I spent in here last year while we were supposed to be in Boys' Foods. We learned that if we sat still and stayed quiet, no one would have a clue that we were there. The place was so big, with its endless rows of darkened seats, that we would just blend in and become invisible. It's like in wartime in the jungle, when the soldiers wear green-and-brown camouflage uniforms because the jungle is totally green and brown. The soldiers just totally disappear into their surroundings and their enemies can't see them.

If I know Rudy, he's already figured out that I'm the shooter. When the shooting started and everyone panicked, I noticed that some people locked their classroom doors before everyone could get in. The kids who were stranded in the hall tried to squeeze into the classrooms where the doors were still open or ajar.

Maybe Rudy and Kathy were left in the corridor, looking for cover. Barinder was probably in the boys' can the whole time, getting high on weed.

If Rudy is here in the theatre with me right now, I wouldn't know it even if he was sitting there eyeballing me, waiting for the chance to jump me and take away my gun. My armpits feel flooded. I look through the rows but it does no good. He would literally be all over my ass before I knew he was there.

This morning, I was just Walter. Last night, when I took a bath and said goodnight to my family, I was still Walter, a fat ugly boy who, one day, might become a slim, handsome man. Rudy and the rest of Boys' Foods met my parents when our class had all the mums and dads over for dinner at the school. My folks wore their Sunday best and I personally served them a meal I had prepared. Our teacher sampled the food, agreed that it was yummy and was happy to give me an A.

So, what's happened to me? How did I go from being the Boys' Food king to the school gunman? It's taken a while. I'd thought about this day when Rudy and I had our bull sessions in Boys' Foods. Of course, I didn't say anything to him about it. He might have gone and told Mr. Brett. Not that Mr. Brett would have done anything about it.

Rudy isn't here, I tell myself. Neither are the cops. Nobody is going to jump up and disarm me. I can't remember how long I've been in this school with this gun, but it seems like forever and a day. I start to think it's weird that the cops haven't busted down any doors or shot tear gas yet, but then I remember the Columbine footage on YouTube. The cops *there* just stood by their squad cars and shot into the school's windows. Also, I think *our* cops are way too pussy to do something as brave as storm a school and arrest a shooter so that many lives will be saved.

I sit for a moment, front-row center, and stare at the empty stage. I enjoyed my fantasy of being Rudy, stuck in that washroom with Kathy, Barinder and Talia. Sometimes I wish I could be Rudy.

Mostly, I wish I could be anyone other than Walter Horton.

Rudy's not here. The cops aren't here. I almost feel like I could slip out the back door, go home and, if the cops show up at my doorstep, deny everything.

But Rudy could be somewhere else in the building. Same with the cops. I'm so full of adrenalin that he or the police could throw open the theatre doors and I wouldn't know what to say or do. Would I shoot Rudy? How about the cops?

If I were smart, I would shoot myself.

But I'm not sure I'm smart enough to do that.

Why not just hide here in the theatre, between rows of seats? Wait till the cops show up and try to take out a few of them before they blow me into the back row. Maybe I should get on my knees and pray, ask God—if He exists, and I'm not sure that He does—to forgive me for every bad thing I've ever done, even though I'm pretty sure He would say, "Uh, I don't think so."

I think for a moment about Vinny, who's the meanest son of a bitch I've ever met. I believe Vinny will always be a bully and a sadist who has hurt many people, and after he dies, he will have a very hard time getting into heaven, if there is such a place. Of course, he's never done anything like come to school with a gun.

I stop at the concession door, reassuring myself that Rudy isn't down here with me. I'm not his problem; he doesn't have to save the school from me. I may be his friend, but he is not mine. If you asked him, he would probably say, "Walter and I had a few classes together. Our teacher stuck me with him in Boys' Foods."

For a moment, I think about the lockdown, and the kids who shut the doors on each other. Why did they think it was OK to say, "I'm safe inside here, but you're not getting in. Too bad"?

This morning, in Biology, Vinny bullied me in front of the rat's cage. I looked to Rudy for help, but he let me down. If I had stood up to Vinny and punched it out with him, would Vinny have stopped messing with the rat's cage? Probably not. Frankly, I think that in many ways Rudy is as big a dick as Vinny.

I can hide here, or I can go into the concession area, even though Rudy may be hiding there, waiting for the chance to disarm me and subdue me till the cops can come and arrest me. Just a little while ago, I nearly had a heart attack when I tried the theatre door. Now I'm standing at the concession door, anxious about what's on the other side.

Chapter Ten

I'M IN. I can't see a damn thing because the concession is even darker than the theatre was. I start running my hands along the wall in search of the light switch. This room has a second door, which opens out into the supply hall, and the supply hall has doors that lead to other parts of the school. Most of the students here don't know about all these doors and hallways, mainly because they don't care. But if your name is Walter Horton and some bullies have threatened to thrash you after school, you know how to get away very fast. For weeks at a time, I've avoided beatings because the bullies could never guess which of the school's exits I would use.

I'm still in the dark. Where is the damn light?

I can smell dust, paint, cardboard, old sweat and a hundred other scents. When I try to step forward or to the side, I hit something like a box or paint can. For a moment I have a mini-heart attack because I'm convinced myself that Rudy is here in the dark, waiting for me.

I give up on the light switch for a moment and try to calm down. Deep breaths don't help. I'm in poor physical condition, so it takes very little to make me sweat, breathe hard and get exhausted. I hold my breath and listen. Rudy's out there. I'm sure of it. Out in the supply hall.

I want to swallow. I want to do other things: Belch, fart, scream, cry. But I stay quiet. Rudy's near. He'll get the cops. The cops will be coming.

On the other side of the door is the supply room, and beyond that are all those classrooms packed with people who think they are safe from fat, crazy Walter Horton. People who thought this would just be another day at school. Maybe they sent each other text messages of love. No one's ever sent *me* one of those.

I know that I fed our pets this morning. I insist on doing it because I figure that if I feed my pets, they will love me. Their love is more than I have ever gotten from other people.

Tomorrow, my pets will get their food from someone else because I'll be dead. They'll forget about me fast enough and start loving their new feeder. Animals are like that. People, too.

Maybe it would be fun if I discovered Rudy lurking around here and shot him in the head before killing myself. We could go into eternity together.

I'm a diabetic who hasn't eaten lately. I'm feeling poorly. I start slamming into things and still can't find the light switch. Is this what death is like? It's really no worse than life.

Chapter Eleven

"WALTER?"

"Kathy?"

The concession light is on. Kathy has a dreamy quality as she looks down on me, smiling. I think she is the most beautiful girl alive.

"You were making all kinds of noise in here. Why didn't you turn on the light?"

"I couldn't find it."

"Sure a lot of junk in here." She tosses aside a few props from our last school play. "You were making all kinds of noise bumping into everything. You've got to be more careful. You might hurt yourself."

"Yes, ma'am." I look around. No Rudy, no cops.

"The light switch is over here. I thought you knew this place like the back of your hand."

"Kathy, it's dangerous for you to be here."

"You need me here with you right now. You need a friend."

"Are you my friend?"

She smiles. "Forever and ever."

I smile and take her into my arms. I bury my face in her neck, her hair. She smells of sweat and fear, which makes her seem more human and more lovable. I breathe it all in, loving her up.

"I'm so afraid for you, Walter. Of what will happen to you now…"

I have the gun in the jacket of my windbreaker. For a mad instant, I think of shooting both of us, leaving the world to think we were tragic lovers or something.

But no. I was born to live and die as fat, pimply, four-eyed Walter Horton. Kathy was meant for college, marriage and motherhood.

"You know what?" I ask. "You and I could make a break for it. I know all the exits in this school. We could bust out of here. We have the ocean just outside, and the mountains, and the woods. We could get lost and nobody would ever find us…"

She offers me a small, sad smile. "Your problems are like a monkey on your back. They would follow you wherever you went. You have to face them and deal with them. Besides, I have my whole life here—my family, friends—"

"Like Rudy."

She shrugs. "He's part of my life, yes."

"Am *I* part of your life, too?"

"If you want to be."

"Do you *really* want to be friends with me? Remember, I'm Walter Horton—fat, pizza-faced, four-eyed Walter."

She purses her lips. "You don't always have to be that person. You can lose weight; people do it all the time. Your skin will clear up. You can wear contact lenses. Mostly, though, you need to learn to like yourself."

"Good luck with that," I mutter.

She nods. "You play the cards you're dealt. I think the game's worthwhile."

We stay silent for a few moments so I can let her wisdom sink in. You play the cards you're dealt, eh? Kathy was dealt a good hand—good face, good body, lots of charisma. She should try spending one day of her life as Walter Horton. Then maybe she would understand me a bit better.

Kathy says, "You know that thing this morning with Vinny and the rat? It wasn't your fault. You mustn't blame yourself."

"I could have prevented the whole thing. I could have saved the babies."

"You tried to save them. If you had tried to prevent Vinny physically, he would have punched you out."

"I hate it that Vinny knows he can bully me and get away with it," I said.

"He'll outgrow it eventually," Kathy said. "Vinny can't go through life pushing and shoving people around and saying, 'You're dead after school.' School ends, and then Vinny and the rest of us will have to find jobs to support ourselves, and no one will hire him if he's got this attitude that's, 'I'm Vinny and I'm a bully. If anyone bugs me, I'll kill them.'"

I still don't think Kathy understands bullies like Vinny or victims like me. Vinny isn't the main reason I ditch school so often. I ditch because, after a while, it seems like the normal thing to do. Staying home from school and watching TV all day is easier than going to school and dealing with all the hassles there. Not to say that ditching is a good idea. It isn't. It's just as easy way of sparing myself the pain of going to school and trying to get along with people who dislike and disrespect me.

I don't want to tell Kathy that today was inevitable. I've known it since the day my dad bought his Glock in case someone broke in. There are many more Walter Hortons in this school, and this world, than anyone realizes. The school shooters in the States—Eric Harris, Dylan Klebold, Kip Kinkel, Rudy Lanze—were all Walter Hortons. A hundred other boys—and girls—at my school could have done what I'm doing today. Maybe they will, tomorrow, next week, or whenever.

—

46

In this school, Kathy is everyone's favorite girl. Whenever she walks into a room, smiling at everyone, people stop what they're doing and smile back. Whenever *I* walk into a room, people ignore me or sneer. Sometimes they'll even say, "Oh, there's fuckin' Walter."

I look into Kathy's kind blue eyes and say, "I wish I didn't have to be me."

Chapter Twelve

The theatre and the cafeteria are at opposite ends of the school. Transporting carts of food from the cafeteria to the theatre could be a big problem if they had to do it past hallways full of students because the kids here lack the good manners to get out of the way or open the doors for the cart-pushers.

To avoid such a hassle, the school has its hidden hallways that make the trip between the theatre and cafeteria fast and convenient. Those hallways have rarely been painted, and the walls are covered with scratches from careless people. The tile floors are full of grime and dirt that nobody ever seems to clean up. That whole part of the school could use new paint and flooring, but Mr. Brett probably thinks that the money and effort could be better used elsewhere. Besides, if the students and general public never see the filth and scratches, who cares?

Kathy takes my hand, squeezes it, doesn't let go. I like that so much. We creep down the halls, cling to the walls, dive between the carts. We've covered enough ground to hear the frightened voices of kids locked inside the cafeteria.

"I think," Kathy says, her voice scarcely above a whisper, "that Walter's somewhere in these crazy hidden hallways. He knows that from here he could easily get into the cafeteria kitchen, and then into the cafeteria. There are no locked doors."

"The kids don't know that," I reply. "If they did, they would do a major freakout."

Together we wait for a moment and breathe hard, then hurry up and wait some more.

Soon we're much closer to the cafeteria. "All these carts," Kathy mutters. We make our way around them and look this way, then that.

I feel so close to Kathy that I don't want this adventure to end.

I don't want to wake up.

Barinder was right: The cafeteria is packed with students. If I wanted a high body count, I could take out lots of my classmates.

But I don't want to do that. I just want to spend as much time as I have left with Kathy. Rudy is probably around here, in this maze of secret passageways, waiting for the chance to relieve me of my firearm.

I walk a few steps more, then hear footsteps. I know that click-click-click, that heavy tread. It can be only one person.

Mr. Brett.

I can hear his voice. He's on his cell. What is he saying? He's probably not ordering a pizza. I'm really impressed that he knows about these hidden hallways and has found his way to us. He's the principal and I'm a nobody, but I have a gun and he doesn't.

I walk closer and closer towards him, wondering what we will say to each other when we meet.

Chapter Thirteen

I SILENTLY SCREAM at Mr. Brett, "Keep talking, big man. Keep it up."

Mr. Brett keeps it up.

Rudy is somewhere around here, probably trying to get Mr. Brett's attention and gesture for him to shut up, because crazy Walter might hear him and move in for the kill. But Mr. Brett talks louder and louder, his voice getting angrier by the second.

Mr. Brett, when at school, is used to saying, "Jump!" and expecting the other person to reply, "How high?" When that doesn't happen, he gets loud, angry and frustrated.

Rudy's just as worried about Kathy, who's here too. She's hiding, probably trembling with fear.

Don't worry, Kathy. I don't shoot girls.

I keep walking along. Then I stop. Through my peripheral vision I can see Rudy right up against the wall, eyeballing me. He probably thinks I can't see him. He probably has lost bowel control by now and can smell his own shit. I don't smell so pretty myself. I have huge armpit sweat stains. I have sweat streaming down my face, too. But then, I'm always sweaty and smelly. That's because I'm fat.

I look ahead and see Mr. Brett. He sees me, too. He drops his cell and stares at me.

I raise my dad's Glock.

Mr. Brett says, "Walter…"

I fire my gun.

Chapter Fourteen

THE GUNSHOT IS so loud that it hurts my ears. I can hear Mr. Brett sobbing. I didn't think he knew how to sob. I'm glad he's still alive. It would be a shame to lose him.

I look back towards Kathy, happy that I've gotten to know her just a little bit. She's probably worried that I'm going to cap Mr. Brett again and go after her. I would never do such a thing to her, though.

I hear some sort of racket and turn around to see Rudy coming to tackle me. I can't get the gun up fast enough, so he takes me down. I'm fatter than he is but he's in far better shape than I am. He could easily take me in any fistfight or wrestling match.

Our struggle is brief but intense. Both of us have such sweat-slick hands that neither of us can get a firm grip on the other. I try to knee him in the nuts, but he blocks my knee with his, and then he starts punching me out.

I've heard it said that just before you die, your life flashes before your eyes. In my case, I piss my pants. Rudy hits me in the face again and again. I howl from the pain and raise my dad's Glock to my temple. Before I can get the bullet into my skull, Rudy gets a grip on the gun, too. I'm in too much pain to put up much of a fight, so now Rudy has the weapon. He maneuvers me onto the floor and points the gun at my face.

"Kathy!" he yells. "Run!"

He looks down at me and I look up at him. I wish he would have the courtesy to shoot me and put me out of my misery. But no.

Kathy just stands there. She points down the hallway, and we see Mr. Brett. Next to him are about a dozen police officers, guns drawn, taking aim at Rudy.

Chapter Fifteen

"DROP YOUR WEAPON! Drop it!"

The cops are here, all of them dressed as if this is Iraq or Afghanistan and they're here to kick some ass. In their blue uniforms and head-to-toe protective equipment, you would have thought they were ready to save people trapped inside a nuclear-power plant during a meltdown, not confront a distraught fat kid who's brought a gun to school.

Problem is, Rudy has the gun. Maybe they'll pop him instead of me. Then they'll have *so* much explaining to do later on.

Rudy looks down at me. If he drops the weapon, as the cops are yelling at him to do, I'll grab it and shoot him or Kathy. I would never shoot Kathy, but Rudy doesn't know that. I could shoot myself and bring this whole drama to a tidy little end.

Rudy shakes his head but says nothing. He probably can't speak. I can see, or at least sense, his body vibrating from terror. I could reach up and try to snatch away the gun, but Rudy wouldn't let go.

I tilt my head so I can see better. The cops don't know who's who around here, so if Rudy doesn't drop the piece pretty soon, they'll spatter his brains and balls all over these nicked-up old walls.

A cop who's almost as tall as Mr. Brett says, "Final warning. Drop it." He moves in closer.

The cop's gun looks like something Arnold Schwarzenegger would carry in a movie. This cop's even got a silencer on his weapon. Barinder knows a lot about guns. If he was here, I would ask him about why this cop needs a silencer right now. Barinder might say,

"It's so that the cop doesn't get freaked out by the sound of his gun when it fires."

The cop's hands seem to shake a bit as he aims his gun at Rudy.

Huge gun. Overstimulated cop. Bad scene.

Rudy blurts, "Not me. Wrong guy."

The cop can clearly see my dad's Glock in Rudy's hand.

"It's not me!" Rudy screams. *"It's Walter!"*

I look this way and that. The cops have come in from both sides of this hidden hallway. One of them springs up from behind us and takes Kathy down in a gentle sort of tackle. More officers assist him in taking her into custody, even though petite Kathy offers no resistance. I shift onto my side to see what's happening, and Rudy pivots. We are surrounded by blue uniforms.

I look up at Rudy, as if to say, *Can you believe this shit?*

Kathy wails. "Rudy's not the one!"

I see other cops emerge. We must have most of the city's SWAT team here today. Maybe they don't understand, or believe, what Kathy has just said. They're all aiming at Rudy's head.

Mr. Brett tiptoes towards us. "Rudy, give me the gun."

I look up at Rudy. He looks at Mr. Brett. He wants to hand over the gun, I think, but can't bring himself to do so.

Mr. Brett says, "It's OK, Rudy. We know you aren't the shooter."

Rudy says, "Do the cops know?"

Mr. Brett points at Rudy and shakes his head. I'm not sure that the cops get the message.

Mr. Brett says, "Rudy, it's OK. It's all over. Hand me the gun."

Mr. Brett says, "Rudy…"

Rudy's grip on my dad's Glock visibly loosens. He is holding it by two fingers. As soon as he starts to raise it, I reach up and try to snatch it away. At that moment, the police start shooting.

Chapter Sixteen

THE ROAR OF gunfire in the hallway is deafening. Then it stops, immediately. The ringing in my ears starts up, reminding me of the last rock concert I went to.

Then I feel nothing.

"Code three-eleven!" one of the cops shouts into his radio.

"Where's Kathy?" Rudy yells.

A cop pats Rudy's shoulder. "She's all right."

He sees her then. She has her face cupped in her hands.

Rudy calls out, "Kathy!" But when she sees him and hurries to hug him, a cop takes her away.

He tries to walk around but his feet slide on the slippery surface. He looks down at me and sees my blood on his clothes. Within minutes, white-shirted paramedics hurry in with a gurney. They rush past me and go to Mr. Brett, who needs medical attention far more than I do.

Rudy looks at me some more. My glasses are twisted and broken and my plastic pocket-protector is gone. That's all right—I won't be needing them anymore.

Mr. Brett is sprawled on the floor, wincing in agony. A cop checks him out, squeezing his thigh. They give him oxygen and put bandages on his wounds.

After a few minutes, one of the cops stops putting pressure on Mr. Brett's wounds. The cop sits back and looks at his blood-smeared hands. I wonder how many times he has had to do this, and if ever gets used to it. doctors see this all the time, but doctors are doctors and cops are cops.

The paramedics ease Mr. Brett onto a gurney and wheel him off to the nearest hospital. Rudy starts looking for Kathy and finds her in a corner with a blanket over her shoulders, huddled like a street girl who hasn't slept in five days. He sits down next to her, puts his arm around her and she rests her head on his shoulder.

A cop comes over, kneels down and wants to ask questions, but Rudy waves him off. The cop nods, like it's OK if they don't want to answer questions now but maybe later. I don't think Rudy or Kathy will ever be ready to talk about what they've been through today.

The cops come over to me, lots of them, checking me out. Maybe they're thinking, *Oh, so this fat little bastard is the cause of all this trouble.* They've taken away my dad's Glock. I hope they give it back to him.

One cop says to the other, "Over a thousand students, one shooter with plenty of ammo, and the only fatality is the perp. Our lucky day."

Amen to that.

Chapter Seventeen

THE BEACH IS quiet at ten in the morning. It's just the way I like it. Mr. Brett looks different in his gym attire. I didn't know he owned that sort of clothing.

"Rudy," he says, "last one of the morning. Run for one minute."

He nods. So do I, sweat pouring all over me, chest heaving, legs burning. He yells, "Go!" and we do just that, even though I hurt more than I could ever describe. I think I'm going to fall down and die by the time he blows his whistle to alert me that my minute is up. Then I start walking.

Running, walking, running, walking. That's my deal with Mr. Brett. I think my "baby fat" is melting off already. Next week I'll be running more and walking less. Within a few months, I may be ready for my first marathon.

I don't go to gym now. Instead, I work out with Mr. Brett and Rudy. On the drive back to school, he says, "Gets easier every day, eh?" I don't agree, but I reply, "Yessir." Even though he can't hear me.

For weeks after the incident, media trucks lined the street outside our school and everyone got his fifteen minutes of fame. Talia had plenty to say to each reporter who wanted a sound bite, and just about all of them did. I think now she wants to go to journalism school so *she* can rush over to locked-down high schools and stick the microphone into the traumatized students' faces.

Talia told ABC, NBC, CBS and CNN about how Kathy and Rudy tried to stop me. But you know something? People think *he* was in on it. They ask him, "How did you know where Walter would be?" Then they say, "You two were friends. Walter was your best friend. He must have told you he was planning this. Why didn't you go to the authorities?"

It's all such bullshit, of course. But the reporters' are there to ask those kinds of questions and get everyone all stirred up.

Some people have even said that Rudy was the one with the gun and he got me killed. Maybe those people have said that because they want to believe it.

After all this happened, everyone had plenty of questions and wanted answers. Even *I* couldn't have provided those answers, and even if I could have provided answers, most people wouldn't have understood those answers.

Afterwards, some students wanted to lower the school flag to half-staff in my memory. Mr. Brett said no, but Barinder did it anyway. I watched him do it. He made me very happy.

For a while, parents started driving their kids to and from school, as if some copycat would continue what I had started. But then life just got predictable and boring again, and kids took the bus or walked to and from school, again.

Those other kids and their families all thought they had come close to losing each other, even though that was never the case. My family lost me that day, and now I see the three of them, my parents and kid sister, having dinner, not saying much to each other. They've cried a hundred times since they learned of my death, but *that* will stop soon enough. They may wonder why they've gotten over my death so fast. I know why. It's because my death was a blessing. I once read an article about an obese, mentally ill woman who'd spent her life in and out of psychiatric hospitals. Her family knew that she would never have a normal life and would always be a burden on them. So when she died of complications related to being really fat, they said, "It's good that she's gone."

Well, that's how it was with my family, especially my father. He was ashamed of me because I would never amount to anything; I was doomed to being fat, pimply, four-eyed Walter who couldn't do anything right. I never thought of my father of being King Shit, either, a man who was no better than I was and never would be.

Very soon, they will raise that flag back up and everyone will start to forget about Walter Horton and what he did that day. In the future, only people with very good memories will say, "Hey! Isn't this the school where that fat kid came with a gun...?"

Mr. Brett says to Rudy, "They didn't even have a memorial service."

Rudy knows he means me. My people don't believe in memorial services or funerals. It's just the way we are.

"The Hortons said they didn't think it would be appropriate to have a funeral, considering how Walter died," Mr. Brett says. Then, "I can't imagine how it must be for them, coping with all this."

I laugh, thinking, *Don't worry about them, Mr. B.*

"I got a call on my cell that morning," Mr. Brett says. "I knew immediately that Walter was the shooter. His mum discovered a letter—"

"A suicide note?" Rudy asks.

"I would call it a will."

Rudy laughs. "I didn't know Walter had any assets to leave anyone."

"No assets. Just a few final thoughts. 'Taking care of business,' as you kids would say. That rat sure meant the world to him. He considered it a family member."

Rudy nods. "Walter left a note about its care and feeding. I'm taking over that job."

"No more ditching?"

"Guess not. Kathy makes sure of that."

Mr. Brett smiles. "I like Kathy."

"So do I," says Rudy.

I like Kathy too. I see her all the time, even though she can't see me. It's better that way.

"Rudy," says Mr. Brett as the three of us enter the main foyer, "if you're going to attend classes and be a good student, I guess I can stop worrying about you and start worrying about Barinder."

"I know where you can find him," Rudy says.

I do, too. Mr. Brett returns to his office. Rudy heads off to his next class and go into the boys' can to watch Barinder smoke weed.

Chapter Eighteen

Instructions for Care and Feeding of Rat

(Her name is Joanie)

Rats are omnivorous, so if there's a food you like, chances are that Joanie will like it, too. Dry dog food is an excellent choice. Feel free to serve her cooked beans but not raw beans or veggies.

Water: Change her bottle often. Joanie doesn't like stale water any more than you do. Never give her pop (rats can't burp).

Cage: Wood chips are fine. Use ones that smell good; replace them once they get funky. Whenever I clean her cage, I put Joanie in my baseball cap that I've taken off and turned upside down. For some reason, she likes to curl up in my cap and watch me make her living space fresh and clean.

Clean her tray with water and a small amount of dish detergent. Don't use too much detergent; she has a much better sense of smell than you do and probably won't like the detergent smell all the time. You don't need to wash the bars of her cage or her wheel unless they get yucky. She enjoys chewing on toilet-paper rolls and making her nest with toilet paper and cotton balls. Whenever I clean her cage, I remove most of the cotton and replace it with fresh. I leave a little bit of old cotton in there so she'll recognize it as her home.

Misc.: Don't be freaked out by her large size. Joanie loves being held and talked to. She'll try to get out of her cage, but doesn't everyone. Remember, rats are living things, too. Treat her the way you want to be treated.

W.H.